Fairy
Unicorns

Cloud Castle

Zanna Davidson

Illustrated by Nuno Alexandre Vieira

Meet the Unicorns

Zoe

Astra

Sorrel

Unicorn King

Nimbus

Orion

Lily

Shadow

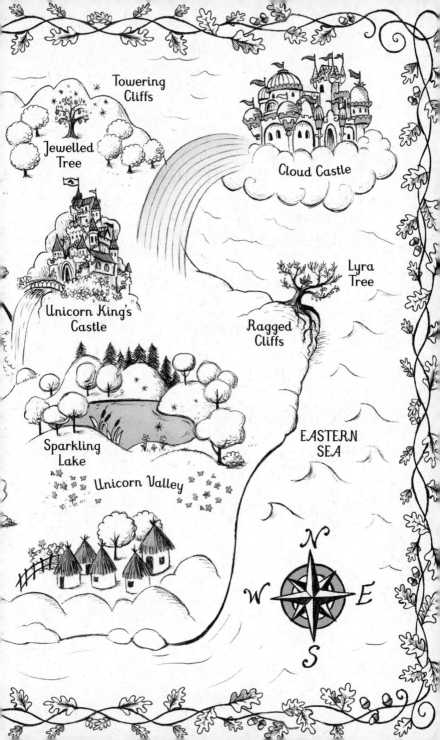

Towering Cliffs

Jewelled Tree

Cloud Castle

Unicorn King's Castle

Lyra Tree

Ragged Cliffs

Sparkling Lake

EASTERN SEA

Unicorn Valley

N
W E
S

Contents

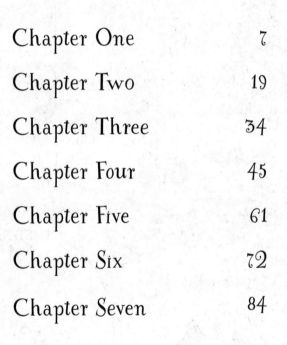

Chapter One

Zoe waited until the clock struck midnight. It was an old-fashioned grandfather clock, with a chime that echoed around the house. On the last count, Zoe crept out of her bedroom and paused for a moment, but all was quiet. Then she tiptoed down the stairs.

She was staying with her Great-Aunt May for the summer holidays, in her tumbledown cottage in the country, and Zoe had soon learned that everything wasn't as it seemed. At the end of Great-Aunt May's garden, hidden inside a tree, was a secret passage to another world…a magical island full of fairy unicorns. And Zoe was going there tonight!

She carefully lifted the latch on the back door and crept out into the moonlit garden. The warm summer breeze seemed to tug her forwards and she made her way down the mossy path to the huge oak tree at the bottom of the garden.

Only when she wa[...]
waving branches did s[...]
tiny flask from her bag.[...]
pinched her fingers toget[...]
herself with its golden, sp[...]

Zoe held her breath. For [a m]oment, she
thought the magic wasn't going to work…
that perhaps she had imagined it all. But
then her toes began to tingle, and so did her
fingertips. She felt a shiver run up and down
her spine…yes! It was happening! She was
starting to shrink.

Her great-aunt's garden soon towered above
her, the long grass now like trees. The tiny gap
between the roots of the oak tree revealed itself
as a tunnel. She was fairy-sized and ready for
her next adventure with the unicorns.

the tunnel's entrance and
red the words of the spell that the
nicorn King had given her:

Let me pass into the magic tree,
Where fairy unicorns fly wild and free.
Show me the trail of sparkling light,
To Unicorn Island, shining bright.

As soon as she'd finished chanting, the
tunnel began to shine with a glimmering light.
Zoe stepped into the oak tree, the ground soft
and warm beneath her bare feet. She followed
the twisting path, until at last she could see
the end of the tunnel, and a glimpse of the
land beyond.

She stopped for a moment and gasped, still

unable to believe the magic of it all. There was Unicorn Island…she could see the little glade and birds swooping through the azure blue sky. She ran the last part, her heart pounding with excitement. Would it be the same? Would it be as wonderful as she remembered?

There were the slender trees, their bark shining with a magical glow, their rainbow leaves fluttering in the breeze. A path wound through the trees, and in the distance Zoe could just make out a lush green valley. Birds swooped and dived around her, their calls like musical chimes. It was even better than her dreams.

And, even more excitingly, there was her friend Astra, galloping out of the trees to greet her. The little unicorn's coat shone creamy

white. Sunlight sparkled over the stars on her
back and her horn glowed like an ocean pearl.

"Astra!" Zoe cried. For a moment she stood
there shyly, then she flung her arms around
Astra's neck, burying her face in her silky soft
mane and breathing in her
warm, honey scent.

"You're back!" said Astra, softly. "I knew you'd come back."

Zoe laughed. "I couldn't wait!" she said.

"And you've come on the best day…it's the Midsummer Festival," said Astra. "There's going to be dancing and feasting and a parade down Moon River."

"I can't wait!" said Zoe. Then a thought occurred to her. "How did you know I was here? I was going to come and find *you*!"

Astra laughed, her eyes twinkling. "Last time you came, there was a strange humming noise in the forest, like bees around a flower. And then today, I heard the noise again. I think it must be the island's way of letting us know someone's coming."

Zoe smiled at her. "Only you would have noticed," she said.

Astra longed to be able to do magic, but she was the only unicorn on the island who couldn't. More than anything, she wanted to be Guardian of the Forest one day, like her mother, and have the magical power to care for the trees. But Zoe thought Astra was special in other ways. She was always working things out, as if she were putting together a jigsaw puzzle in her mind.

"Oh!" said Astra suddenly. "Before I forget, I've got something for you."

She cantered over to a grassy mound and came back with a beautiful flower wreath. It was made of ivy and twisted round with wild roses, wood sage and bluebells.

"It's to wear at the Midsummer Festival," she said, shyly.

"Oh!" gasped Zoe. "It's lovely. Thank you! But what about you?"

Astra grinned and disappeared between the trees for a moment. When she returned, she was wearing a trailing cloak of honeysuckle and a necklet of wild strawberries.

"I love it!" cried Zoe, clapping her hands in excitement. "You'll be the best dressed

unicorn there!"

Astra smiled but shook her head. "Just wait until you see the Flower Unicorns," she said. "Their costumes are always the best."

On her last visit, Astra had taught Zoe a little about the magical world of Unicorn Island. Zoe had discovered that there were several kinds of unicorn who each helped the Unicorn King look after a different part of the island. The Flower Unicorns lived in the meadows and cared for the flowers and insects.

The Snow Unicorns kept to the mountains and looked after the animals of frost and snow, while the Cloud Unicorns lived in the Cloud Castle – a floating palace in

the sky, where they tended
to the birds and the clouds.
Then there were the River
Unicorns to watch over the
creatures of the water, and
the Forest Unicorns, like
Astra, who cared for the
trees and the woodland animals.

"Oh!" cried Zoe. "I've never met a Flower
Unicorn. Will there be lots of unicorns there?"

"*Everyone* comes to the Midsummer
Festival," said Astra, and smiled as Zoe
clapped her hands in excitement. "Now climb
on my back, and we'll fly together."

As she spoke, she bent her knees. Zoe
swung herself on to Astra's back until she was
sitting astride the little unicorn with her legs

tucked neatly behind Astra's wings.

"I hope I remember how to fly," she said, suddenly feeling nervous.

"You will!" said Astra, confidently. "I'll start off slowly for you."

Astra beat her gossamer wings and soon they were soaring up, up, up into the sky.

"Oh!" cried Zoe, clinging on tight. For a moment she felt giddy, watching the ground rush away from her and seeing the treetops pass beneath her feet. But then she remembered the rhythm of Astra's flight, the way she powered her body forwards, the feel of the wind rushing through her hair, and she relaxed into it.

"I'm flying again," she whispered to herself. "I'm really flying!"

Chapter Two

They soared over the Silvery Glade where
Astra lived, beyond Fairtree Forest, and into
Unicorn Valley. Snow-capped mountains
towered majestically in the distance and
below them, the sparkling Moon River wound
its way across the lush green of the valley
floor. Zoe could just make out smoke pluming
from one of the mountains far on the horizon.

For a moment, she flung out her arms, loving the feel of the breeze against her cheeks, breathing in the warm summer air. The day was heating up fast and Zoe could feel the sun's rays pricking her skin.

"It's not far," said Astra, picking up speed as she sensed that Zoe was beginning to relax. "The Midsummer Festival is just beyond the next bend in the river."

As Zoe gazed down at the beauty of it all, she couldn't help a little shiver at the thought of her last visit… An evil pony called Shadow had put a curse on the island, attacking the trees and imprisoning the Unicorn King. Shadow had come from Fairy Pony Island, across the sea, and was determined to take over Unicorn Island and rule it himself. They'd only just managed to thwart him last time. What would happen if he struck again?

"Shadow hasn't come back, has he?" Zoe asked, cautiously. "Or done anything since I was last here?"

Astra shook her head. "He still has our precious book of spells, the Grimoire. He knows that by our laws, if the island is destroyed, then the King will have failed in his role and can no longer rule. We're all worried Shadow will try to destroy the island again. But he hasn't struck so far… I just hope he's given up."

"Oh! Me too," said Zoe.

They rounded a little hillside, and then all thoughts of Shadow flew from Zoe's mind as the Midsummer Festival came into view.

"Oh! I can see it! I can see it!" she cried, leaning forwards in excitement. Below her, on the banks of the Moon River, were beautiful tented stalls, garlanded with flowers and topped with brightly coloured flags.

The unicorns were gathered around the stalls, their butterfly wings shimmering, their horns glowing in the sunlight. Some were dancing to a unicorn band, their hoofs flashing in time to the music, while

others performed magical feats, disappearing and reappearing in a shower of sparkles.

Astra glided down gently onto the riverside grass and Zoe slipped from her back, her smile nearly reaching her ears.

"Look on the river," said Astra.

Zoe turned to see yet more unicorns sailing down the river in golden boats. They were dressed in flowery costumes, with long trains and towering headdresses.

For a moment Zoe just

gazed at them, enjoying the view and the cooling breeze from the river.

"I'm glad we're by the river," she said. "It's so hot here today."

"I know," Astra replied, a faint frown creasing her brow. "I don't think it's ever been this hot on the island, even at Midsummer. Let's go and try the ice creams – we'd better get there before they all melt!"

At the sound of their voices, one of the unicorns turned, and Zoe saw that it was Astra's mother, Sorrel.

As she came towards them, Zoe felt her calm, magical presence. It was as if she always carried something of the quiet green stillness of the forest with her. She had threaded woodland flowers through her mane and tail, and a train of honeysuckle decorated her back, sweeping the ground as she walked.

"Welcome back, Zoe," she said, her voice soft and wise. "I'm so glad you've come. Astra and I were hoping you'd be here in time for the festival."

"Thank you!" said Zoe. "And is the Unicorn King here?" she asked, eagerly. "I'd love to see him again."

But Sorrel shook her head. "We heard word that Shadow is on a neighbouring island, and the King has gone to investigate. Hopefully he'll return in time for you to see him. Now," Sorrel went on, "the only rule for today is that you enjoy yourself. There are honey cakes and sparkling nectar juice and flower blossom sweets among the stalls. I'm sure Astra will show you round."

"It sounds delicious!" said Zoe.

"Then let's eat!" said Astra, grinning at her.

They wandered through the stalls, feasting on cakes and honeycomb ices, while Astra pointed out the Snow Unicorns, who had come down from the high mountains, and the Flower Unicorns, who were surrounded by clouds of butterflies wherever they walked.

And all the time, the sun seemed to burn
brighter and brighter.

"I wish there were at least *some* clouds," said
Astra. "Otherwise the festival will
be ruined. We haven't had the costume
competition yet and all the flowers will have
wilted by then."

As she spoke, she pointed towards a beautiful
unicorn with the most
amazing costume
of them all.
It was made
entirely of delicate
flower petals that
fluttered from
her body as
she moved.

"That's Lily, Guardian of the Flowers," said Astra. "She always spends weeks planning her costume."

Zoe noticed that Lily was casting anxious glances at the cloudless sky. Then she trotted over to Sorrel, and the two Guardians bent their heads in deep discussion.

Zoe looked around the festival and saw several more unicorns huddling together, talking in hushed voices. "Astra, is something wrong?" Zoe asked. "Everyone seems nervous – as if they're waiting for something to happen."

"I don't know," said Astra, slowly. "Maybe it's just the heat…" She scanned the crowds as she spoke. "I know what it is," she said, suddenly. "It's the Cloud Unicorns.

They're missing!"

"Are they the ones who live in the Cloud Castle?" asked Zoe. "Maybe they've stayed there because of the heat."

"That wouldn't be enough to stop them," said Astra, shaking her head. "They always come down for the Midsummer Festival; that must be why everyone's worried."

"Is there anything we can do?" asked Zoe. "Could we fly to their palace?"

But Astra shook her head.

"I think we should just wait," she said. "I feel too hot to fly! Let's take shelter under the trees. I can feel my coat beginning to burn."

They ducked beneath the branches. Soon, more and more unicorns came to join them, to escape the fierce rays of the sun. Some of the unicorns swished their tails from side to side, desperately trying to stir up a breeze.

Then a unicorn near them looked up at the burning sun and muttered, "Maybe this is Shadow's work."

At the sound of his name there was a ripple of fear through the crowd and Zoe felt another pang of unease.

"Up there!" cried another unicorn suddenly. "Look!"

Zoe followed his gaze to see what at first looked like a dazzling, shimmering cloud, gliding down from the sky.

As it came closer, Zoe realized that it was a band of unicorns, their wings beating in time, hooves pounding through the air, a trail of dust glittering in their wake.

"Oh!" Astra gasped with relief. "It's the Cloud Unicorns. They've come after all."

As they touched down in the valley, Lily, Guardian of the Flowers, stepped forwards to meet them.

"Greetings," she said. She looked at the largest unicorn, with a gleaming coat, who wore a shimmering circlet on his head, and

Zoe guessed he must be their leader.

"Nimbus," said Lily. "Why have you come so late?"

"We've just had a message from Shadow," said Nimbus, his voice grave with warning. "He's struck again. He's using the Grimoire to wreak yet more terrible magic. And this time…he's stolen the clouds."

Chapter Three

As soon as Nimbus had finished speaking, there was uproar among the unicorns.

"This is terrible," said Sorrel. "Without the clouds, there will be no rain, and all the plants will die."

"And there will be nothing to shield us from the sun," said Nimbus. "We are all in grave danger."

"We can't let this happen," said Lily, shaking her head. "The flowers are the most delicate. They'll be the first to die. We *must* find the King."

"We may not be able to reach him in time," said Nimbus. "We all know the prophecies written in the Grimoire – once the island reaches a certain heat, there's no turning back. I'll send someone in search of the King. The rest of us must find the clouds, and fast."

"But they could be anywhere!" said Astra.

Nimbus shook his head. "The King has cast a banishment spell. Shadow has the Grimoire, so he can still cast spells on us, but he can't come to the island himself, nor can he steal anything from it. The clouds must be hidden somewhere on the island."

The Guardians huddled together, talking in urgent whispers. Zoe and Astra crept closer, but all they could hear were snatches of conversation. "…could be anywhere…", "under the ground…", "locked away". The loudest voice came from a large unicorn with glittering hooves and jet-black eyes, who looked oddly familiar.

"Who's he?" whispered Zoe.

"That's Orion," Astra answered. "Guardian of the Spells. We met him before at the Unicorn King's Castle."

"Of course," said Zoe.

As if sensing her interest, Orion turned and gave her a hard-eyed stare.

"Oh!" said Zoe. "He looks so angry."

"Don't worry," Astra replied. "He's never

been the friendliest of unicorns. He seems to
think his knowledge of spells makes him more
important than the rest of us."

At last, Nimbus broke away from the
group and pounded the ground three times
with his hoof. At once, everyone fell silent.

"We've decided that the Cloud Unicorns
will search the island, with the help of the
Guardians. We will look in the White

Mountains, in the forests and valleys, and we'll talk to the River Unicorns, to see if they have found anything. Everyone else, please find shelter and shade and stay safe until we can get the clouds back."

"But first," said Orion, "I suggest that the Guardians drink this potion. It will add to your powers and speed your wings. As Guardian of the Spells, I always carry a little with me, for times of emergency."

"Thank you," said Nimbus.

One by one, the Guardians of the Flowers, Trees, Clouds and Snow stepped forwards to take a sip of the potion.

"There is one place no one must go," added Eirra, Guardian of the Snow. "Long ago,

Mount Flores was a volcano. It has been dormant for many years, but this morning we noticed it was active again, with smoke pluming from its chimney. I want to warn everyone to stay away from it."

"Thank you," said Nimbus. "And as for the Unicorn King—"

"I'll go!" said Orion, stepping forwards quickly, his coat gleaming in the harsh sunlight. "After all, I am one of the swiftest unicorns and I know where to find the King."

Nimbus nodded, but before he could do anything else, Orion began to beat his huge, gossamer wings. A moment later he was soaring across the sky.

"Astra! Zoe!" called Sorrel, as she trotted over to them. "I must return to the forest, to see if the clouds are hidden there, and also to look after the trees. It's vital we keep them well-watered, so they don't suffer too much. I want you two to stay here by the river. It's the safest place for you to be. You can shelter beneath the trees and drink from the river. Whatever you do, please *don't* try to help. Shadow is a dangerous and powerful pony. We don't know what he may do next, or what traps he may have set."

"But we want to come with you," protested Astra.

"We helped last time," added Zoe.

"No," said Sorrel, firmly, shaking her head. "It's much too dangerous. The Guardians are the most skilled unicorns on the island and the Cloud Unicorns are helping us already.

It's our job to try to fix this – not yours.
Now, I must go…"

She briefly pressed the
tip of her nose
against Astra's,
then rejoined
the other
Forest Unicorns.

Together, Zoe and Astra watched as the
Guardians and Cloud Unicorns began to
leave, taking to the air in graceful, powerful
wingbeats, until everything was silent once
more.

The heat seemed more intense than ever
and Zoe realized that all the flowers from the
festival had already wilted, drooping
sorrowfully from the stalls.

She turned to Astra, a flash of determination in her eyes. "We can't just sit here," she said. "We have to do *something* — make a plan!"

"I agree," said Astra. "I did have a thought — Shadow must have hidden the clouds in the last place anyone would look. We just need to think where that might be…"

"If only I knew Unicorn Island better," said Zoe. She gazed around, hoping for inspiration to strike. "What about the river?" she asked.

Astra shook her head. "The River Unicorns would know if Shadow had cast a spell in their home." As she spoke, her gaze rested on the volcano, smoking in the distance.

"Don't you think it's odd," she said slowly, "that the volcano, Mount Flores, has become

active on the same day

as Shadow steals the clouds?"

"I don't know," said Zoe.

"It could just be a

coincidence."

But when she turned to look at Astra, she could see the excitement on her face.

"I'm not so sure," Astra went on. "A smoking volcano is the *last* place anyone would look…"

"Well then," said Zoe, catching hold of Astra's excitement. "We've got our plan!"

"Hang on," said Astra. "I didn't mean that *we* should investigate the volcano. Because that's about as dangerous as it gets…"

Zoe grinned at her friend. "I think that's exactly what we should do."

Chapter Four

Astra fixed her eyes on the distant volcano, watching the smoke plume up into the cloudless sky. "I'm really not sure investigating the volcano is a good idea…" she began.

"You know it's our best shot," Zoe pleaded. "Come on, Astra. If it's too dangerous, I promise we can turn back."

Astra took a shaky breath. "Okay," she said.

"Mount Flores, here we come."

Zoe and Astra carefully took off their costumes before Astra bent down so that Zoe could get on to her back. As soon as Zoe was sitting comfortably, Astra began beating her wings, powering them up into the sky.

Zoe looked down at the beautiful island and knew she had to help. It wasn't just the flowers that were suffering. Already the grass was beginning to look tired and brown, and the higher they flew, the hotter the air became.

The sky was eerily empty as they neared the volcano, with no birds to join them in their flight. And without the clouds, everything seemed strangely still. The glare of the sun was hot on their backs and Zoe's throat began to feel dry and parched.

Mount Flores was easy to spot. There was a narrow opening on its rocky peak and thick smoke rose from its chimney. Astra flew straight towards it, scything through the air with powerful wingbeats.

"It smells like real smoke," said Astra, as they drew near. "And it *looks* like it… Maybe this is a very bad idea. I'm not sure I want to fly into a volcano."

She hovered for a moment in the air, as if ready to turn back.

"But the smoke could just be one of Shadow's spells, couldn't it?" asked Zoe. "That way, he might have thought no one would look inside it."

"Or it's a real live volcano and it's about to explode," Astra pointed out.

"Hmm," said Zoe. Then she shook her head. "But we've come this far. Let's just go to the top and see. I promise we can turn back then."

Astra had to laugh. "Okay! But if it starts spouting out fire, I'm out of here."

"Agreed," Zoe promised.

Astra circled the volcano once, looking for a place to land. Then she fluttered down and perched on a little ledge on the volcano's rim.

"Well, at least it's not hot," said Zoe. "That has to be a good sign."

They stood for a moment, watching the smoke rise into the air above them and then drift away.

"Maybe there's only one way to find out," said Zoe.

"I think we're going to have to fly down into the volcano."

Astra leaned forwards, gazing down into the volcano's abyss. "It does look a long way down," she said.

"The Snow Unicorns said that Mount Flores hasn't been active for years," Zoe replied.

"I've got a good feeling about this."

"Zoe!" said Astra. "Even if you're right, and Shadow has hidden the clouds here, remember what my mum said. Shadow is dangerous. This whole thing might be a trap."

"Do you want to turn back now?" Zoe asked.

"No," Astra replied. "I just don't want to put you in danger."

"You're not putting me in danger," said Zoe. "I know the risks – I just think they're worth taking."

Astra shut her eyes for a moment. "And I thought I was a sensible unicorn..." she said.

She opened her eyes again. "Okay," she went on, as if steeling herself for what was to come. "Jump on my back and hold tight. Let's do this."

Without another word, she leaped forwards. In a flash, they had left the world behind them and were plunging down into the swirling darkness. The deeper they went, the colder it became. It was like an endless black tunnel, and the crater at the surface became smaller and smaller until it was just a pinpoint of light.

"Look!" said Zoe, as Astra held out her wings to slow their fall. "The smoke has gone!"

"Yes," said Astra, fighting for breath. Even with her outstretched wings they were still descending at speed. "That's very…reassuring."

Their fall seemed to go on for ever. Zoe was just wondering if the volcano was somehow bottomless when Astra began beating her wings again. "Here goes," she said. "We're about to land."

A moment later they hit the ground and Zoe tumbled from Astra's back, landing with a bump on a sandy floor.

"Oops," said Astra. "That was sooner than I'd thought."

Zoe blinked up at her. Only a tiny crack of light from the surface reached them down here. She looked around; it seemed they were in a shadowy chamber with fine-grained black sand and darkly glittering walls.

"Oh no!" said Zoe, standing up. "I don't think there's anything here. I can't see any sign of the clouds, can you?"

"No," Astra replied. "Although it's hard to see anything in this darkness. But I don't understand it…if the smoke was just a trick, why isn't anything hidden here?"

"Maybe Shadow did it to waste our time," said Zoe, despairingly. "So we'd *think* the clouds were hidden here. I'm sorry, Astra," she went on. "It's all my fault. We should never have come here."

Zoe went to the back of the chamber and sat down with a bump, then let out a cry as she landed on something hard.

"Ow!" she said. And then, "Ooh!"

"What is it?" asked Astra, racing over to join her.

As their eyes adjusted to the dim light, they could just make out a casket in front of them. Zoe whooped with excitement. "It's got to be... hasn't it?"

Astra bent for a closer look. "Yes!" she cried. "Look! Can you see them? The wisps escaping from under the lid. We've found the clouds, Zoe!"

Zoe flung her arms around Astra's neck and hugged her tight.

Then came a voice from the darkness behind them. "Not so fast…"

Zoe and Astra turned as Orion stepped out from the shadows.

Zoe gazed at him for a moment in confusion. "But I thought you went to fetch the Unicorn King?" she said. "How did you get back here so quickly?"

Orion smiled at her. There was something in the way he looked at them that filled Zoe and Astra with unease.

"No," he replied. "I never went to get the King. Why would I do a foolish thing like that?"

"What do you mean?" asked Astra. Her unease had turned to fear, and Zoe could hear her voice trembling.

Orion let out a low laugh. "Come on," he said. "A clever little unicorn and a human girl should be able to work it out."

Astra took in his expression, the way he was gloating over the casket of clouds, and gasped. "Are you… are you on *Shadow's* side?" she asked.

"Of course I am," Orion sneered. "Why would I want to follow a weak king?"

"He isn't weak!" protested Zoe.

"Oh, but he is," said Orion, rounding on her, and she could see his coal-black eyes glittering in the darkness. "That's why I'm helping

Shadow. He could do wonderful things for this island! The Unicorn King never allows us to practise Dark Magic or have fun with our unicorn powers. And now Shadow has the Grimoire, there's no telling what he can do."

"But our king is good," said Astra. "He cares for the island. He works hard to protect us all."

Orion laughed. "Who cares about *good* when there's so much power to be had? And as soon as Shadow takes over, he's promised to share it with me."

"I see it now!" said Astra quietly, as if talking to herself. "You're Guardian of the Spells. You must have stolen the Grimoire *for* Shadow. And then you were so quick to offer to find the King. You didn't want anyone else telling him what was going on, did you?"

"That's right," Orion boasted. "I even sent the King off in the first place, looking for Shadow, so we could have fun with this little spell while he's away. But do you know what?" He stepped closer until he was towering above them. "I'm actually glad you two found the casket of clouds. You ruined our plans last time, and now," he laughed, "I can make sure you won't be able to do it again."

"What are you going to do?" asked Zoe, trying to hide her fear.

"I'm going to keep you here," Orion said, his voice cutting through the air. "Since you don't have magic, you'll never be able to escape… By the time they find you, it will be too late for your precious king. Shadow will be the ruler of Unicorn Island for ever."

He turned around, grabbed a net from the floor in his strong, sharp teeth and then began beating his wings, spiralling up the volcano. When he reached the top, Zoe and Astra heard a faintly muttered spell. There was a crackle of purple-green light and then Orion was gone. But the top of the crater was covered in a thick, black net.

"Quick, Zoe! Onto my back," said Astra.

"The net…" said Zoe, as they flew up towards it.

"There must be a way through," said Astra.
But when they reached the top, it seemed
there was nothing they could do to shift the
net. Astra tried biting through its thick twine,
and Zoe pulled at it with all her
strength, but it held fast.

"Orion must have sealed it with a spell,"
said Astra. "We really are trapped. And how
is anyone ever going to find us?"

Chapter Five

Zoe felt as if the darkness of the volcano was closing in on them, pulling them back down to the bottom. She opened her mouth and shouted as loudly as she could. "Help!" she called. "HELP!"

"No one can hear us," said Astra. "We're miles from anywhere. And Eirra told everyone to stay away from the volcano – remember?

Our voices just won't carry that far."

Astra stretched out her wings and they glided back down into darkness. Once at the bottom, they gazed despairingly at the criss-crossed bars of the net, which closed off their escape and blocked what little light they had.

"What are we going to do now?" asked Zoe, trying to keep the worry from her voice.

The air smelled musty and dank, nothing like the sweet scent of the Midsummer Festival. It was as if they really were in a prison and Zoe had no idea how they were going to escape.

"Outside it must be getting hotter and hotter," Zoe went on. "We've got to let everyone know that the clouds are here."

She took a deep breath to still her rising panic and looked around, wondering if there could be another way out. Then her gaze rested on the casket in the dim light. "Unless," she said, "there's a way *we* can free the clouds?"

Astra eyed the casket doubtfully. "It's sure to be locked by a spell," she said. "Orion isn't Guardian of Spells for nothing."

"It's worth a go," said Zoe. "Let me try." She slid her fingers beneath the lid and heaved. Nothing. There were no locks, nothing that seemed to prevent it from opening, but the lid still wouldn't budge.

"I can't do it," said Zoe. "You have a go."

Astra bent down and tried to prise off the lid with her teeth, but again, nothing happened. In frustration, she kicked the lid as hard as she could, then whinnied in pain.

"It's useless," she said. "It is sealed with a spell. *If only* I could do magic, then we might have a hope of freeing the clouds. Instead we're stuck down here in this prison. And the island is running out of time. I'm sorry. This is all my fault."

"No, it's not," said Zoe, peering to see Astra as she paced around the darkened chamber. "After all, I was the one who pushed us to come here. We can think of a plan. We *must* think of a plan."

Astra stopped pacing, but only long

enough to answer. "Neither of us can do magic. We have nothing with us. There isn't *anything* we can do. And it's all my stupid fault for not being able to do magic."

Zoe had never seen Astra this angry before. She was stamping her hoofs, pounding the ground in frustration, her long silky tail swishing from side to side. Zoe sensed she was close to tears and she racked her brains for a way to comfort her.

Then she noticed something…

"Astra," she said, almost in a whisper. "The silver stars on your coat…they're glowing. Has that ever happened before?"

Astra turned her neck so she could see. "No," she said. "At least, I don't think so."

"And there's something else," said Zoe.

"The air around you, it's sort of…fizzing and filled with tiny sparkles. I've only seen that once before, when the Unicorn King cast a spell. What does it mean?"

"I don't know," said Astra, breathlessly. "I feel strange. Different, somehow."

"Oh!" said Zoe. She'd had an idea, but she hardly dared to voice it, in case she was wrong. "Astra, you don't think this means you *can* do magic, do you?" she asked.

"How could it?" said Astra. "I've never been able to do magic before. But this feeling…"

"Quick!" said Zoe, rushing up to her. "Try something! Try to open the casket!"

"I don't…I don't know *how*," said Astra, staring at the casket. "I've never cast a spell before. And if Orion has locked this casket, he will have used the strongest spell he knows. I won't have the power to break it, even if I can do magic."

"Do you know *any* spells?" asked Zoe, gently.

Astra's eyes flashed and Zoe knew she'd had an idea. For the first time, she began to feel hopeful that they'd find a way out of the crater, and have a chance of saving the island.

"What is it?" she asked.

"I do know a spell," said Astra. "It's a very

small one that my mother tried to
teach me a long time ago. It might just work.
Come! Quickly, before this feeling goes."

She bent her legs and Zoe leaped onto her
back. They spiralled upwards, towards the
top of the crater, and as they flew, Astra
began to chant a spell:

> Come air, crackle with light,
> Come sparkles, shining bright.
> Shoot like an arrow way up high,
> Write my message across the sky.

As soon as Astra had finished chanting, a
flurry of glorious sparkles shot from her horn
and, like a firework, made a trailing, blazing
arc across the sky.

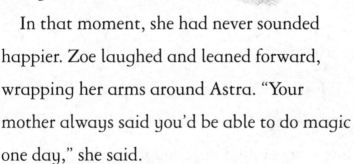

"It's working, it's really working!" gasped Astra, as they hovered beneath the net. "I made a spell! Can you believe it?"

In that moment, she had never sounded happier. Zoe laughed and leaned forward, wrapping her arms around Astra. "Your mother always said you'd be able to do magic one day," she said.

"Now wait," said Astra, a look of pure joy on her face. As the sparkles began to fade, they left behind a message, written large across the sky. It read:

The clouds are hidden inside Mount Flores Come quickly

"Wow!" said Zoe.

"I know," said Astra, with a grin. "I wrote a sky message. I don't know how long it will last – hopefully long enough for the Guardians to see it."

"That's amazing!" cried Zoe. "We're saved! Well done, Astra. You did it – you used magic. You really did!"

They grinned at each other, but Zoe's smile suddenly faded as another thought occurred to her. "Oh no! What if Orion sees the message first? I don't suppose you could cast another spell…to get us out of here?"

"I can't," said Astra. "I think my magic is all used up."

Zoe glanced down at Astra's back and noticed that the stars on her coat had stopped glowing. "Maybe it's because you're so new to it," she said. "Perhaps it will come back."

"I hope so," said Astra. "But now we just have to hope the Guardians find us…before Orion!"

Chapter Six

Astra and Zoe hovered by the entrance to the volcano, Astra nervously fluttering her wings as they scanned the skies for any movement. The message had slowly faded from view, until only a few golden sparkles were left.

"Oh no," said Astra. "I don't think my spell lasted long enough. And now I don't have enough magic for any more."

As she started dropping down the tunnel again, Zoe took one last look up at the sky. "Wait!" she cried. "What's that – in the distance?"

With new hope, Astra found the strength to keep fluttering her wings as they scanned the skies.

"Yes!" she cried. "That glittering streak. It must be…it is! It's a Cloud Unicorn and he's heading this way."

As he came closer, Zoe could make out Nimbus, Guardian of the Clouds, followed by the other Guardians – Sorrel, Lily and Eira.

"We're in the volcano!" cried Astra. "We're trapped under the net! And the clouds are in a casket at the bottom!"

In a beating of strong, glimmering wings, the Guardians landed on the rim of the crater.

"Astra! Zoe!" gasped Sorrel. "How did you get here? I asked you both to stay by the river."

"I'm sorry," said Astra. "We were trying to help. I just had this feeling that the clouds might be in the volcano, and we had to try it out. And, Mum…it was me who wrote the sky message. I did magic!"

Despite her frown, Zoe could see that

Sorrel's face was alight with pride. "We'll talk about this later," she said. "First, we need to get you out of here. There's just one problem…"

"What is it?" asked Zoe.

Sorrel took a deep breath. "We've lost our magic," she said. "All of us."

"But how?" asked Astra. "I don't understand."

"We think it was Orion," said Nimbus. "Much as we hate to doubt him, we all drank his potion before he left. And from that moment on, none of us have been able to do magic. It's the only explanation we can think of."

"It *was* Orion," said Zoe. "He's working for Shadow now. He trapped us in the crater!"

The Guardians exchanged solemn glances.

"Then it's just as we thought," said Lily, Guardian of the Flowers. "He has betrayed us. But we cannot stop, just because our magic has gone."

Zoe could see from the Guardians' expressions that they weren't used to having to solve problems without magic.

"Could you try using your strength instead of magic?" Zoe asked. "If Astra flies further down the tunnel, maybe you could break the net with your hoofs?"

"We can certainly try," Nimbus replied.

"Okay. Hold tight, Zoe," said Astra.

She stopped beating her wings and they glided gently down the tunnel.

Looking up, Zoe could see that the
Guardians had gathered right at the crater's
edge. At a word from Nimbus, they began
pounding the net with their hoofs.

The strands began to break away.

"It's working!" Zoe cried.

At last, the net was hanging by a thread.

Sorrel gave it one last kick and the net fell to the side. A moment later, Astra rose from the crater on her shining wings, and fluttered down to land beside the Guardians.

"Good thinking, Zoe!" said Sorrel, smiling at her. "Now we just need to work out a way to free those clouds."

But as she spoke, there was a blast of wind and they were all blown backwards. Zoe and Astra tumbled over rocks and stones, finally skidding to a halt behind a large boulder, some way from the crater's edge.

Blinded by the smoke from the volcano,

at first it was impossible to tell what had happened. But as the smoke cleared, they saw Orion hovering above the volcano, his huge wings furiously beating the air.

"Stay back," Sorrel whispered to Zoe and Astra. "Don't let Orion see where you are."

Astra and Zoe crouched low behind the boulder and watched, quaking, as Nimbus flew towards Orion on outstetched wings.

"Traitor!" cried Nimbus. "How could you betray us like this?"

"I betrayed you because when Shadow rules this island, I'll rule with him," Orion snarled. "I'll finally have the power I deserve."

"You won't get away with this," said Nimbus, flying towards him.

"Won't I?" said Orion, laughing. "I think

you'll find you're too late. Your time has nearly run out. Soon the heat will be enough to destroy the island, and by Unicorn Law, the King will no longer be able to rule this land. Then it will be Shadow's turn."

"You've chosen the wrong side, Orion," Nimbus went on.

"I don't think so," said Orion.

Before Astra and Zoe's horrified eyes, he lowered his horn. A bolt of lightning flashed out, and struck Nimbus in mid-air.

The Guardian of the Clouds froze, as if he'd suddenly been trapped by invisible walls.

The next moment, Sorrel, Lily and Eira charged towards Orion, but without magic, they too were powerless against him.

One by one, Orion struck them.

They hung, motionless in the air, their heads thrown back, anger flashing in their eyes.

Zoe heard Astra gasp. "My mother..." she said, her voice choked with sobs.

"What's Orion done to them?" Zoe whispered.

"He's used Dark Magic," Astra replied. "It can freeze a unicorn so they can't speak or move…" She stopped, unable to go on.

"It's going to be okay," said Zoe, trying to soothe Astra as she stroked her soft coat. "The King will come back. He'll set the Guardians free again and release the clouds. Maybe if we can just hide here until he comes…"

But she wasn't sure she believed her own words. Orion was looking gloatingly at the Guardians. And surely it was only a matter of time before he spotted their hiding place?

Astra was shaking with anger beside her. "I can't believe Orion's done this," Astra said. "I've got to stand up to him."

"Astra, no!" cried Zoe. "We've still got to save the clouds!" She tried to hold Astra back, using her arms like reins, but it was no use. Astra darted out from their hiding place and

flew straight towards Sorrel, as Zoe clung on to her.

Orion saw them at once and glowered at them. "There you are," he said. "I'll see to it that you never interfere in my plans again." And he raised his horn to strike.

Chapter Seven

Orion's face was pure fury. As she looked at
him, Zoe felt herself trembling in fear.
Instinctively she held up her arm, as if to
block his spell, and closed her eyes. But
nothing happened. She could feel Astra
quivering beneath her, making no sound. Zoe
dared to open her eyes...and gasped.

A fireball was hovering in front of them,

burning so fiercely that Zoe could feel its heat. But it wasn't coming any closer. Something was holding it at bay.

And then Zoe realized that Astra's magic had returned. The stars on her coat were glowing, her horn was lowered and all her energy and focus seemed to be poured into that fireball, as she fought to hold it off.

Orion's horn was lowered too and he was muttering spells under his breath, desperately trying to drive the fireball towards them. Zoe stayed as still as she could on Astra's back. She could only watch and hope that Astra's magic stayed strong.

You can do it, Astra, she thought, silently urging her on. And then, like Astra, her gaze locked onto the fireball, and she could feel her

thoughts focusing on trying to push it back.
Her fingertips began to tingle, as if some of
Astra's magic was coursing through her veins.

For a moment, it felt as if they were
winning, but then the fireball began inching
closer towards them. Zoe could tell by Astra's
slowing wingbeats that she was tiring.

"Ha!" said Orion. "Do you really think you

can beat me on your own, Astra? You don't
stand a chance. I can tell you're weakening.
Give up now."

"No," whispered Astra.

"And if you do," Orion went on, "I'll make
sure you're rewarded when Shadow becomes
our ruler. Look at Nimbus. Pathetic. Even
your own mother couldn't stand up to me."

At the mention of Sorrel, Astra threw back

her head and pointed her horn at the fireball
once more. The tingling in Zoe's fingertips
grew stronger. She could feel Astra's fury, and
once again her own gaze locked on the
fireball, urging it onwards.

This time, it kept going –
rocketing back
towards Orion.

He let out a cry of
shock and fear as he
dodged it, then swivelled
round, raising
his horn to
strike again.
But then, as

he looked at Astra and Zoe, a strange mixture of fear and awe crossed his face. The next moment, he was gone, getting smaller and smaller as he sped across the sky.

"We did it!" said Astra. "We really did it."

"I know," said Zoe, still unable to believe that Orion had really gone. "But why did he fly away from us? I was sure he was going to stay and fight…and then something made him change his mind."

"I don't know," said Astra, but her voice sounded weak.

Zoe bent down to stroke Astra's neck, and only then did she realize how exhausted Astra had become. Her body was trembling all over and her wingbeats had become feeble.

"Quick," said Zoe. "You need to land."

Weaving slightly from side to side, Astra made her way to a ledge halfway down the volcano. Zoe slid from her back just as Astra crumpled to the ground.

"The clouds…" she said. "With the Guardians still trapped, who is going to release them? This will all have been for nothing…"

Zoe tried to soothe Astra, gently stroking her silky mane, but inside she was beginning to feel desperate.

Gazing across the island, she realized, for the

first time, the damage caused by the burning sun. She began to feel just how intense the heat had become.

The snow on the mountains was melting fast and water was gushing down the slopes, taking with it huge boulders. They were smashing into trees and flattening plants. Lower down the slopes, the grass, once so lush and green, now looked yellow and withered. And there was no sign of wild flowers in the meadows.

"All this time we've been in the volcano, the heat has been destroying the island," Zoe said, tears coursing down her dusty cheeks.

"Perhaps we've run out of time."

"No, we haven't," said Astra. Her voice was still weak but a slow smile was spreading across her face. "Look!" she whispered. "We're saved! We're saved!"

Zoe followed her gaze and saw the Unicorn King flying towards them on his wide wings, his crown glinting in the sunlight.

The King lowered his horn, and with a single bolt of blue light, he freed the Guardians from their frozen prisons. Without pausing, he swept into the volcano. A moment later, there was a booming sound. Then the clouds burst from the top of the volcano and began streaming far and wide across the sky.

As the sun was blocked from view, Zoe

felt a wonderful cooling shade. Then the
King appeared again, standing on
the top of the crater. His body seemed to
swell for a moment and then he
breathed out, long and loud.

A fine mist streamed from his
nostrils and covered the clouds,
which swelled and darkened and
then burst into rain.

Cheers echoed from down in the valley, as Unicorn Island began to spring back to life.

When Zoe next looked up, Sorrel was at their side.

"Are you all right?" she asked, gently.

They both nodded.

"Are you?" asked Astra.

Sorrel nodded. "The King's spell has

returned our magic. We were all deceived by Orion. I still can't believe he's betrayed us like this."

Astra nuzzled close to her mother.

"Mum," she said quietly. "I fought off Orion. I really can do magic – powerful magic."

Astra looked over at Zoe as she spoke.

"I've realized something else too," she added. "I think I can only do magic when I'm with you, Zoe. There's something about you being with me that makes it happen. Did you feel it too?"

Zoe thought back to the moment when she'd focused on the fireball, and the strange tingling she'd felt in her hands.

"Yes," she said. "I really did."

"Maybe all this time, your magic was waiting for Zoe to arrive," said Sorrel, smiling at them both.

Then she nuzzled her daughter to her side.

"I always knew you had magic in you," she said.

"That's not all," said the Unicorn King,

joining them. "I've never seen a unicorn this young with such strong powers. And Zoe, I think you must have been sent to help us in our time of trouble. Once again you have worked with Astra to save Unicorn Island. I want to thank all of you, for protecting the island while I was away."

"How did you know to come back?" asked Zoe.

"I had my suspicions about Orion," replied the King, "so I asked my old friend, Magus, to keep an eye on things. As soon as he heard about the clouds he came to find me, not trusting Orion to do the job. I came back as fast as I could. I imagine Orion will have gone to join Shadow now, but at the very least he no longer has our trust. I can only hope our island will be much safer."

"And now," the King went on, "it's time to celebrate. I know the Midsummer Festival was ruined by the heat. I can think of no better place to hold it now, than among the clouds." He looked at Nimbus as he spoke, who smiled in return.

"Come, all," said Nimbus. "Follow me to Cloud Castle. I'll write a sky message as we fly, inviting everyone."

"Can you fly?" Sorrel asked Astra. "Aren't you exhausted after using your magic?"

"I'm not sure," said Astra. "I think I can feel my strength coming back to me, but my wings still feel so weak."

"Zoe, come and fly on my back," said Sorrel.

"And I'll support you if you need it," added

Lily, smiling at Astra.

They followed in Nimbus's
wake as he led
them in a dancing
spiral, up through
the airy blue. Zoe
had to hold on
tight as they flew.
They were rising at
such a steep angle that if
she'd let go, she would
have slipped straight
from Sorrel's back.

As they soared through the
clouds, Unicorn Island
disappeared from view.
Everything was silent and
muffled as the wispy whiteness of
the clouds washed over them.
Then they broke through
and Zoe cried out in delight.

Floating just above them, held up by pure
magic, was a gleaming white castle. Its
soaring turrets were topped with flags, which
fluttered in the breeze. It was encircled by
curling wisps of cloud, like a beautiful sky
garden.

"I've never been to this palace before," said
Astra, flying beside her. "It's so high up you
can't see it from the valley. I think it might be

the most magical of them all."

Nimbus led them in through a rainbow
archway and then they all touched down on
the soft white floor of the palace courtyard.

The Unicorn King glanced around the
room, golden sparkles fizzing from his horn.
He looked at a table and, in a flash, it was
laden with food. Then he touched the

waterfall in the corner, turning its water to

sparkling juice. Next, he let out a

long, low whistle and a flock

of birds flew

through the window,

carrying bells, harps and

triangles.

A moment later the

castle was filled with

beautiful music.

Zoe watched it all, feeling as if

she was in a dream. Then, hearing the sound

of wingbeats, she and Astra ran to the window

and looked out. Flying towards them, through

the blue sky and rolling clouds, came unicorn

after unicorn.

The Flower Unicorns came first, dressed in

their beautiful costumes, and Zoe saw that the flowers had sprung back to life, glowing with colours even more vibrant than before.

"And to think Shadow nearly won," said a voice behind her.

Zoe turned to see the Unicorn King, gazing through the window with them.

"But we stopped him," said Zoe.

"Do you think he's going to try again?" asked Astra.

The Unicorn King looked grave for a moment. "I do," he said. "Shadow isn't one to give up easily. But together, I'm sure we can defeat him."

When the Unicorn King left them to greet the other unicorns, Astra turned to Zoe. "I want to say thank you," she said. "Without you I might have never been able to do magic."

"Well," Zoe replied, "without you I wouldn't have such amazing adventures. We really do make a great team."

They grinned at each other. "Now let's
enjoy the festival," said Astra, "before
it's time for you to leave."

It was night before Astra winged her way back across Unicorn Island as Zoe sat peacefully on her back, gazing up at the stars above.

"They're so close," said Zoe. "I almost feel I could touch them." Her hand trailed behind her, through the dark warmth of the night sky. "I never want to leave," she added sleepily.

"Then you'll come back again?" asked Astra, as she touched down at the entrance to the Great Oak.

"I'll be back," said Zoe. "I promise."

Astra smiled. "I'm glad," she said. "I think Unicorn Island needs you. And I do too. You've taught me how to do magic."

"It wasn't me," protested Zoe. "I know

nothing about magic!"

"We'll see!" said Astra, smiling.

Zoe gave Astra one last hug and then ran down the tunnel, back to her own world.

Another wonderful adventure, she thought to herself. *I can't wait for the next one to begin...*

Enter the world of the

Fairy
Unicorns

and collect every
enchanting tale

Magic Forest ISBN: 9781474926898

Zoe is staying with her great-aunt when she discovers
a magical world full of fairy unicorns – hidden at the
bottom of the garden. But Zoe soon finds out that
Unicorn Island is in terrible danger.

Cloud Castle ISBN: 9781474926904

Zoe and her friend Astra can't wait for the
Midsummer Festival. But Unicorn Island is
growing hotter and hotter… Has Shadow,
the evil fairy pony, stolen the clouds?

Coming soon...

Wind Charm ISBN: 9781474926911

When Zoe visits Unicorn Island she mistakenly opens the
Box of Winds, unleashing a terrible storm over the island.
Can Zoe and her best friend, Astra, the fairy unicorn,
stop the winds before it's too late?

Enchanted River ISBN: 9781474926928

When Zoe discovers the island is flooding, she knows
she has to stop the waters – and fast. Is there any way
for Zoe and her best friend Astra, the fairy unicorn,
to save the island from disaster?

Frost Fair ISBN: 9781474926935

Winter's arrived on Unicorn Island, and Zoe can't
wait to visit the Frost Fair with her best friend Astra.
But when cursed snowflakes begin falling, the unicorns
are turned to ice. Who could be behind this evil plan –
and can Zoe and Astra stop them?

Star Spell ISBN: 9781474926942

The time has come to defeat Shadow, the evil fairy
pony, once and for all, and Zoe returns to Unicorn
Island to help. But her best friend, Astra, is in
terrible danger, and only Zoe can save her...

If you've loved Fairy Unicorns, why
not enter the world of the

Midnight Escape
ISBN: 9781409506287

Holly is staying with her Great-Aunt May when she
discovers a tiny pony with shimmering wings. At first
she thinks she must be dreaming…until two fairy
ponies visit her with an urgent mission.

Magic Necklace
ISBN: 9781409506294

Holly and her friend Puck are visiting the Pony Queen
when a magical necklace is stolen from the palace.
Can Puck and Holly help track it down before
the thief uses its magic?

Rainbow Races   ISBN: 9781409506300

Holly can't wait to watch her friend Puck compete in the
Rainbow Races. But when an enchanted storm is
unleashed over Pony Island, ruining the races, the home
of the fairy ponies is threatened with darkness for ever…

Pony Princess   ISBN: 9781409506379

When the Fairy Pony Princess comes to visit, Puck and
Holly are given the all-important job of looking after her.
But then their royal guest goes missing. Can Puck
and Holly find her again?

Unicorn Prince   ISBN: 9781409506362

Holly and Puck uncover a wicked plot to take
over Pony Island. To save the day, they must
venture into the Enchanted Wood, home of the
mysterious unicorns…

Enchanted Mirror   ISBN: 9781409506386

Pony Island is in danger. The ponies are losing their
magic and the Pony Queen's powers are under threat.
Can Holly and Puck uncover the mystery of the
missing magic, before it's too late?

Edited by Becky Walker

Designed by Brenda Cole

Reading consultant: Alison Kelly

First published in 2017 by Usborne Publishing Ltd.,
Usborne House, 83-85 Saffron Hill, London EC1N 8RT, England.
www.usborne.com

Copyright © Usborne Publishing, 2017

Illustrations copyright © Usborne Publishing, 2017

Front cover and inside illustrations by Nuno Vieira Alexandre

The name Usborne and the devices 🎈 🎈 are Trade Marks of
Usborne Publishing Ltd.

A CIP catalogue record for this book is available from the British Library.